WIDER
THAN THE
SEA

Serena Molloy

WIDER
THAN THE
SEA

Illustrated by **GEORGE ERMOS**

HODDER CHILDREN'S BOOKS
First published in Great Britain in 2023 by Hodder & Stoughton

1 3 5 7 9 10 8 6 4 2

A CIP catalogue record for this book
is available from the British Library.

ISBN 978 1 444 96841 5

Typeset in Trebuchet MS by Joana Reis
Printed and bound in Great Britain by
Clays Ltd, Elcograf, S.p.A.

The paper and board used in this book
are made from wood from responsible sources.

MIX
Paper from
responsible sources
FSC® C104740

Hodder Children's Books
An imprint of
Hachette Children's Group
Part of Hodder & Stoughton Limited
Carmelite House
50 Victoria Embankment
London EC4Y 0DZ

An Hachette UK Company
www.hachette.co.uk

www.hachettechildrens.co.uk

**For my mam
and
for yours**

WHAT ONLY I CAN SEE

I watch the **RAINDROPS**

dapple the window

as Mr K sits back

feet crossed on his desk

    like he's at the flippin' beach.

The classroom's *warm* and stuffy

stinks of

    boy-sweat

        and **DAMP** grass

           and someone's pasta pesto lunch.

Afternoon-quiet settled

        over all of us.

I stare at the window

each blob of water *glistens*

when the sun comes out.

And in my head
I start to connect the **RAINDROPS**
 like those join-the-dot pictures
and slowly
 slowly
 something begins to appear.

Mr K glances round the room
asks for volunteers
 the try-hard hands shoot up.

Carefully I slide my notebook out
from beneath my **Small World** book
and sketch the leaping *dolphin*
 made from the shimmering **DROPLETS**
 that only I can see.

Listen to the words
 different voices reading
droning on and on
 fancy towns and cities
 places far from here.

Then

      silence.

No more hands go up.

His eyes move over us

     slide along our row

tight feeling in my tummy

sink low in my chair

     hide behind the boy in front

and try to make myself

not

here.

Inside I'm saying

     not me

     not me

     not me

feel the heat

rising

spreading over me

think of all the ways

I can get out of this

ones I haven't used before.

Glance up.
    A mistake.
'Cos I catch his eye
know he's about to say my name
see it on his lips.

But then
       r   e   l   i   e   f

the home bell goes
       he closes the book
       has already forgotten
            about me.

I breathe out
and know that I'm okay
          for another day.

ASKING ALEXA

One time, I asked Alexa what shyness means.

> Not at ease in the company of others, easily frightened or timid

she said.

At school, people think I'm shy.

But here's the thing

I'm not shy.

I'm not shy.

I'm not shy.

SUNNY DAYS

Saturday morning
Me and The Bean*

(*Real name: Cian

Description: mop of red curls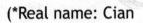

Second name: Hynes!

Always, always destined to be: The Bean)

down past the weir
pedalling like
   our lives depend on it.

Crunch of early **autumn** leaves
beneath our tyres
then clamber
on to the rocks
looking out to **sea**
   and wait   and wait
to see if he appears.

And then   he does.

'Over there, Ró!
Sunny's over there.'
The Bean stands up
        legs all skinny in those flappy shorts
points out into the bay.

Big and **blue** and **dark** and **glistening**
the bottlenose dolphin curls into the air
shooting like a wingless bird.

Then arches back
into the **ocean**
tail **SPLASHING**
slapping

        the surface
            a spray
        of white foam .
            EXPLODING.

Again

    closer now

        he shoots up

            out of the **waves**

                higher this time

                      his body   twists

                      and turns

                      like one **GIANT** muscle

            so much power

    he almost somersaults

landing backwards

with a massive

slap

then sliding

down

into

the

water.

Again   and again   and again
he loops across the **sea**
curve after curve
of shimmering body
then disappears behind the rocks.

Nothing but the rise of **waves**
we watch
     we wait
hoping for more
 always wanting more
but this time just a nose
     then a head rises up
he looks at us
mouth open
     like he's smiling
then he turns
     and softly swims away.

Now we know that all is well
me and The Bean cycle back

through our small town

stop at Spar for Smooches

with caramel and Smarties and marshmallows

all piled on top

big smiles on our lips

that drip

with little rivers of sticky white

wishing we might

stay like this

not wanting today

to ever   **ever**

end.

TV DINNERS

Dad does sausages and chips for tea
again.

Mam works evenings
at the chocolate factory
which means we get loads
of freebie bars and sweets.

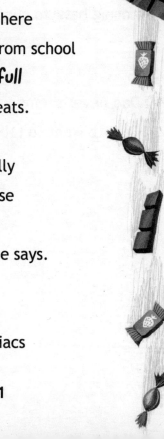

But I'd rather have Mam here
when I get in from school
than a fridge **crammed full**
of all those chocolate treats.

We eat in front of the telly
but Dad still makes me use
a fork to eat my chips
'We're not orangutans' he says.

Don't bother telling him
orangutans are the brainiacs

11

of the primate world
can use all sorts of fancy tools.

He eats his chips
too loudly
lets on he wants to watch the news
but I know that isn't it.

We eat in here
so we don't have to chat.

Lately
Dad never seems
to want to talk
to me.

HOLES

Mr K asks Mya O'Donnell
to hand the new books out.
She acts all surprised
like we don't know
    it's always her he gets to do the jobs.

She slides mine
    too hard
so that it skids
    and slips
    and **PLOPS**
on to the floor

a fake grin tight
on her silly face.

Pretend not to care
pick up the book
open it.

And then I do the thing I always do
　　　　　skip forward to the end
　　　　　check bottom right
233
each page a weight
pressing down on me
flick through it
searching for the blank pages
a picture even
maybe just a map
anything to make it easier
better
less impossible.

There's nothing.

Turn the book over
try to read
what's written on the back

UnberthheatottheTeexansun thereisaqlace
thatissofartom evvverywhere,aqlace
wheeremonowantzto

The letters
        too tightly packed
                all fighting with each other.
'Let's get cracking'
Mr K says
tells us to open our books
        and read the first ten pages
to ourselves
while he writes questions
on the board.

I find the first page
and now a load of words
        DANCING
                and *spinning*
        and **WIGGLING**
every single one

laughing

laughing

   laughing
at me.
I want to tell this Sachar fella
I already hate his **STUPID** silly book

would	*LOVE*
to	take
it	
outside	
and	*dig*
dig	a
big	fat

HOLE

and bury it
   forever.

16

ASKING ALEXA

Alexa says **STUPID** means

> lacking in common sense, perception,
> or normal intelligence.

I'm not stupid. I'm not stupid. **I'M NOT STUPID.**

But then
why does it sometimes feel
like that's   exactly

what I am?

QUID PRO QUO . . .

Mr K says
is when two people
help each other out.

The Bean helps me with homework
and in return I let him play my Xbox
'cos his mam won't buy him one.

But my mam and dad let me have most things I
want
so long as we all pretend
everything is fine at home
　　　　like it used to be.

Quid pro quo
a fair deal for all of us.

Maybe.

SOMETIES . . .

sitting here at the back of the class
I pretend I have a *magic* cloak
it shimmers and shines
and sparkles
CRACKLING with
electricity
wrap it tight around me
and slowly slowly
I start to fade away
till there's
nothing
left
at
all.

CONSOLATION PRIZE,
NOT

The Bean used to play soccer

with the other boys on yard

but he got tired of always being

the last one picked

of pretending to not see

the rolling eyes

only there to even up the teams

so he asked to sit with me

on the low wall

where I go

to draw.

I told him

he talks too much

but inside I kind of liked

not sitting on my own at lunch.

BROKEN THINGS

I used to think it was my eyes
that made the words all **BLuRRY.**

One day this nurse came to check our sight
and said I'd perfect vision.

Then I began to figure it all out
make the pieces fit together

it was me that was the problem
          the thing that didn't work.

I am the broken thing.

MANGA

Me and The Bean sit on the rocks
scoffing sweets and crisps
the Atlantic Ocean **CHOPPY** and **GREY** today
a fishing boat, a blob of colour
way out in the bay.

'He's older than my da, you know'
The Bean says.

'Hem?'
I'm sketching in my notebook now
not really listening.

'Sunny, he's like, 40 or something.
Really old.'

'That's a hundred in human years' I tell him
'the ones in captivity live even longer.'

'Don't go all girl-splainy on me, Ró' he says
but I can tell he's kind of impressed too.
'How d'you know all this nature stuff anyways?'

I shrug. 'YouTube. And *Blue Planet*.'

He looks at what I'm drawing.

'That's so cool' he says
stuffing his mouth with crisps
then tilting his head this way and that
        trying to see
'So what is it?'

'Manga' I say.

'Heh?'

'Japanese animation.'

He asks to see

so I let him take the book
only 'cos he's The Bean
and best friends are meant to share
                    most things.

'You've loads of them' he says
flicking through the pages
trying to make sense of the sketches.
I take it back
                    before he has time
                        to work the story out
that's hidden in the pictures.

'I think he knows it's us' he says
calling out the dolphin's name.

'It's 'cos of the cortex' I say.

'The what?'

'The cortex.'

He shrugs

giving up.

'Whatever, Ró

but I reckon he definitely knows it's us.'

I think about telling him

it's the part of the brain

that makes them clever

but don't want to sound like a pain

or make him feel **STUPID**

for not knowing

so I say

     nothing.

The Bean gets up and starts to whistle

I put my notebook down

go and stand beside him.

The dolphin comes in close to us

     shoots up into the air

     spinning

nose pointing
like a curvy arrow
then slaps down
SPLASHING us with icy *water*
salt on my lips
my face.

He rises up again
straight now
like he's walking on his tail
and *chirps* and *squeaks*
at us.

'See. I told you he was brainy, Ró
I was right.
He SO knows it's us.'

'Yeah, yeah.
You were right'
I say
smiling at Sunny

and The Bean

and I'm laughing now
really laughing
    but only on the inside.

HOLES (AGAIN)

Lying in the dark
>headphones on

listening to that sing-song Texan voice
>up and down

like waves out on the ocean
>soft and harsh

both at the same time
>telling me the tale

of this boy
>called Stanley.

Imagine how alone he must have felt
>the scalding heat of that dry desert

and all those pointless holes to dig.

Only told Dad a sort-of lie
>that I needed the audio book for
>school.

Picked a moment when he wasn't listening

which wasn't hard

'cos mostly he looks busy

thinking   thinking   thinking

like the things inside his head

are way more interesting

                than me.

Except that isn't it.

The things inside his head

must be quite bad

'cos they only ever seem

to make him

sad

       sad

              sad.

Like maybe

              he's

the one with

a great big hole

deep

D
O
W
N

inside his

heart.

ROLLING THE DICE

Mr K decides to test our maths.

Someone passes out the sheets

so many wiggly numbers

       inky worms in a sea of white.

I look at the first ones.

)A(-5 > <̲ 8-

(D(7D>- >01

)⁄0 20< > < -13

Those greater than and less than signs

I hate the most

won't stay put

      they flip

        they flop

not able to decide which way to point

making it all

      impossible.

Numbers **dancing** up and down
turning on the page
        like they can't stay still
and my head starts to hurt
        each sum a little sting
digging into me.

Do what I usually do
        copy someone else's
but Jakob
        who always lets me see
is out today.

        The Bean's too far away to help.

Mya sees me looking
        gives me a manky sneer
and pulls her arm over her work
so I can't see
        one
                single
                        thing.

32

At least it's true or false

fifty per cent chance of being

right

but

fifty per cent chance of being

wrong.

All I can do is roll the dice

and hope my luck

comes in.

OTHER PEOPLE

Keep it hidden in my bedside drawer.
Sometimes late at night
    before I go to sleep
I take it out
    unfold it like a secret.

We're on a beach in Spain
I'm maybe four or five
Mam holding one hand
    Dad the other.

Remember that hot sand
how it burned my toes
    me jumping up and down
dreaming about fancy ice creams
fat bottles of Orangina.

A man with a giant camera
click–click *click–click* *click–click*

snapping passers-by

    when they're not watching.

I look at us back then

    all freckly from the sun

    and happy

like spying on other people.

But the weird thing is

Mam and Dad aren't looking down at me

or into that big thick camera lens

    they're smiling across

just   GAZING **GAZING GAZING**

at each other.

If they did that now

like they want to kiss

on the lips

I'd make a silly face

pretend it was too gross

but inside

I wouldn't feel like that

'cos inside I'd just be

really

really

happy.

PERFECT THING

Sitting on the low wall
with The Bean.
I'm drawing and he's moaning
about his big embarrassing family.

Two annoying sisters
and one pesky little brother.

'You've no idea, Ró
how awful it is.'
He munches on the Rolos
I've brought him from home.
'Nothing's ever yours
always partly someone else's.
I'd love to be like you

THE ONLY ONE

the centre of everything.'

How do I explain

that isn't how it is

that being   **THE ONLY ONE**

means every **STUPID** hope

    every tiny wish

        every mad dream

all depend on you.

Two parents   one child.

How do you tell them

      you're not this perfect thing?

BAD LUCK

Mr K gives back the maths tests.
Mya holds hers up
    just high enough
so everyone behind can see
how well she's done
    all her answers
              spot-on.

At break
I get The Bean
to scribble Mam's name
    he pretends not to look
    at my marks
then shove it in the bottom
of my messy bag
so no one at home will ever know
    how I have done.

ASKING ALEXA

Alexa says **FAILuRE** is

> when someone is unsuccessful or
> disappointing.

Seven out of twenty-five

both

uNSuCCESSFuL

and

DISAPPOINTING.

CRACKS

Today
    when I come into the kitchen
Mam and Dad stop talking.

Think I don't notice
    the weird silence
        the cross words
still hanging
like angry ghosts
    in the chilly air.

They pretend nothing's wrong
make their voices go all chirpy
        like they're on some bad sitcom.

But I can see it all.

Remember Mr K showing us this photo once
an earthquake

the ground all ripped   apart.

Imagine that great big crack

opening up

between them now.

How do I make sure
none of us

F
    A
       L
         L
           S

in?

SUNNY LOVE

The boat wobbles as I climb on
sit beside The Bean
as his Uncle Pat
    rows out into the bay.

Sky and **water**
almost the same blue-grey
like one has leaked
    seeped into the other.

No wind today
so we glide through the **water**
    like sliding across ice.

Pat lets us take the oars.

At first
we're rubbish
    keep butting the ends

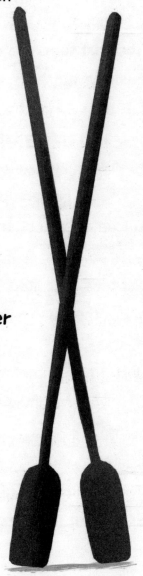

43

against each other
laughing at ourselves
all giddy
        and silly.
The boat turns in a circle
going nowhere
but then we get the hang of it
find a sort of rhythm
        working together
                pull and push
till we're back on track.

Pat tells us to stop
slides the oars up into the boat.

Just drifting now
        water lapping against the **WOOD**
waiting.

The gentle ripple of *water*
as we spot the dorsal fin

cutting through the grey-blue
    moving closer.

Can see his body
a dark shape
    BLURRY beneath the surface
as he circles
slowly
    like he knows
going too fast
    could topple the boat
        hurt us.

A flash of all-knowing eye
as he moves closer
    with each go-round.

Hear his high-pitched cry
    like a baby's
but softer
    soothing
        musical

and the **clicking** sounds he makes
like he's talking
        just to me.

I kneel down
pull up my sleeve
and slip
        my hand
                my arm
into freezing **sea**.

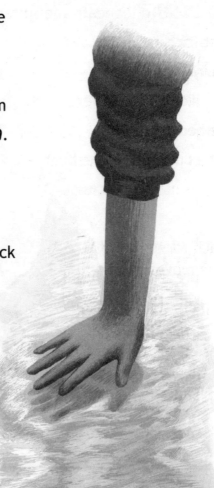

And then
        he's there
rolls on to his back
        for me
white belly
        up
touch his skin
        soft
like velvet

but also
    strong
and smooth
    like nothing else
I've ever felt.

Wait for him
to circle past again
    slower this time
like he wants this
just as much
    as me.

Reach for his belly
    press my hand to it
my palm touching him
    skin against skin
        together
and it's like

somehow
 we already know
somehow
 we have always known
each other.

IF . . .

I could be a superhero
I know which one I'd pick.

I'd be that fella
who freezes things
     makes them stick
       exactly
         as they are.
Stuck
   in a thick layer of ice
         forever.
Maybe
if I can make everything stay
        still
so nothing changes
not
one
little
bit

then Mam and Dad will be okay

        I will be okay.

I'm not a **superhero**

but maybe I can do this.

At least

        I have to try.

SHOPPING

'This would look lovely on you, Ró'
Mam says holding up a purple top
with a fluffy llama on the front.
'You wear too much dark stuff
like those what-you-call-them kids
the vampire ones.'

'You mean goths, Mam.'

'So pale, they look like they never go outside.
A splash of colour's always nice.'

'Maybe' I say
putting the top back and thinking
I might like to be a goth one day.
I don't tell her the top is way too babyish
that all these clothes are for younger kids

                                      than me.

Don't want to hurt her feelings

make her feel sad

again

'cos this morning

when I came downstairs

she was sitting at the table

hands tight around her mug of tea

staring into it

like there was a secret message

written there.

When she looked up
the edges of her eyes were **RED** and **RAW**
like maybe she'd been crying
but I've only seen her cry the once
when Grandad died
so then she had a reason to be sad.

Behind us
I hear someone *laughing*.
It's Mya O'Donnell
in the teen section
with her big sisters.
She's chewing gum
    mouth open
so everyone can see
    how cool she is
and messing with her sisters
trying to seem older
    like them.

And they look so **happy**

together

like they all belong

together.

Don't want Mya to see me here
like this.

Tell Mam I want to look at the hats
and quickly we move away
but inside the feeling doesn't stop
the one that's niggling at me
like a little bit of grit
stuck inside your shoe
and even though you walk away
you still feel it
pressing there.

NOOBS

Ms Flynn, the assistant principal
calls the girls into her room.

We sit in a circle
as she gives us the talk
             about growing up.

Mya straightens in her seat
                 like she already knows
                              it all.
She's wearing one of those crop top things
neon yellow
under her white polo
             no jumper on
even though it's flippin' **FREEZING** in this room.
She sticks her chest out
so everyone can see her noobs
(nearly-not-quite-boobs)
                 like she deserves a prize.

I look down at my flat-as-a-pancake chest

                                relieved

'cos it means

everything is staying

     the same

               exactly

               how I want it to.

Try not to listen

as Ms Flynn goes on and on

about this being 'a time of change'

                       everything 'in flux'

                           'out of our control'.

The radiator makes a funny ticking noise

like it's fighting to come on

so I focus on that

instead of Ms Flynn

and her annoying talk

about these things

I can never let happen.

'Now, girls' she says
finishing up
'if you've any other questions
I'm sure your mams will help'
but in my head
I'm thinking
if I never talk to anyone
about this stuff
it means I'll get my wish
that everything will stay
just as it is.

As we file out
Ms Flynn is fiddling with the radiator
trying to turn it on.

She smiles at me and I smile back
'cos I managed to not hear
most of what she said
so now I'm thinking
maybe I do have a tiny **superhero**

somewhere
inside
of me.

STANLEY, STANLEY

Mr K talks about the desert
tells us he used to teach there once
kids who were way better behaved
               than us.
He asks who's done the homework
               read the first five chapters.
Don't tell him
I'm more than halfway through it all
listening to that Texan voice
late at night
     pulling me into Stanley's story.

When Mr K asks about the name
brings it up
               big and bold
on the white board

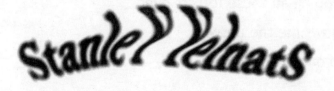

I look at the **WIGGLY**
            squiggly letters
try to make them
stay still
want them to stop *dancing*
the whiteness of the board
            dazzling me
making my head hurt.
But I keep trying
      pushing back
pin those letters down
      fight and fight
the dizzy feeling
hold the letters steady
until
            I   see   *it.*
For once
my **STUPID** brain
flipping all those letters over
shows me the answer
no one else can see

Stanley's two names

    are the same

his surname

   is

Stanley

  backwards.

Want to put my hand up

'cos I know I'm right

but I'm not brave enough

instead I mutter it

    under my breath

hoping Mr K will hear

but he doesn't.

Mya hears

  shoots her hand up

and gives the answer.

MY answer.

Mr K tells her she's spot on

so clever for seeing

what no one else did

and she's smiling

pretending to not

      lap up the praise

he pours on her.

And inside I'm **SHOUTING** –

it was my answer

not hers.

And I'm wondering why she

      who has so much

        who has everything

had to take this one

      tiny thing

        away

from me.

WHEN . . .

I hold a pencil in my hand
have a blank page in front of me
it's like none of the other stuff
matters anymore.

When
my brain can see the picture
imagine it there already
it's like a spark of *magic* lights up
deep down in me.

GIRL AWESOME . . .

is the name I gave my manga girl.

In my sketchbook

I draw her awesome life.

Girl Awesome

lives in an **awesome** house

in the **awesome** part of town

with **awesome** parents

and those two **awesome** sisters

gives **awesome** answers

gets **awesome** marks

wears **awesome** clothes

has **awesome** hair

an **awesome** smile

awesome teeth

awesome flippin' everything.

Of the millions of words

in the English language

I think **awesome** is

the one I hate the most.

WEEKEND RITUAL

Dad lets me crack the eggs
into the bowl and
        poof
a little cloud of flour rises up
tickles my nose
            like I might sneeze.

Add the milk
and stir
till it becomes a stodgy
                soggy batter.

Dad's job
to dollop each ladleful
on the pan.
His hands are wide
        big as shovels
and always stained in the creases
with oil from the garage.

My job
to spot the swiss cheese moment
to flip the pancakes over
when the little holes appear.

We've done this most weekends
for years
sometimes chatting
about nothing
sometimes
a *happy* quiet
like a blanket
wrapped around us.

But today
neither of those is true.

When I shout 'swiss cheese'
and flip
he doesn't smile

like usual
and he doesn't seem to hear
when I prattle on
about how gross
the boys at school are
                    farting all the time
and how Mr K
pretends he doesn't notice
when his face says he does.

Today
        even though Dad's right here
beside me
and I can smell that mix
of petrol and sweat and oil
                        Dad's smell
it feels as though
we're miles and miles   apart.

MS CLEVER-EYES

No Mr K
        today
in his place
a smiling woman
with big hair
       who manages to wear
every colour of the *rainbow*
        in one go.

Tells us her name
is Ms C
and she will be
teaching us
       for a while.

Someone asks
where Mr K has gone
'Sick?'
   'Off having fun?'

'Run away'

        'back to the desert?

to teach those posh kids

        for loads of dosh

who are way nicer

        than us?'

Ms C

will not be pulled

into

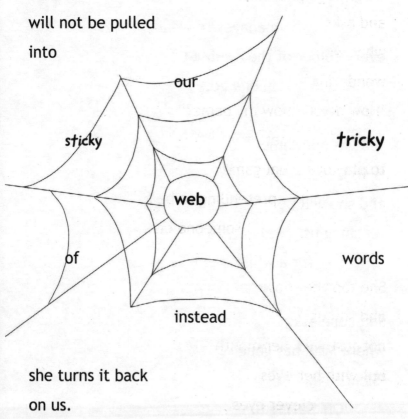

our

sticky   *tricky*

web

of   words

instead

she turns it back

on us.

'No need to pry into
other people's business'
she says.
            Tells Seán to put
his football down.
He stares
            and frowns
and asks
what we're all
wondering
'How d'you know my name?'
'cos we were set
to play our usual game
                pretending to be
                    someone else.

She taps her nose
and smiles
not just with her mouth
but with her eyes
            clever eyes

71

that seem to have
tiny fires
burning **BRIGHT** —
inside.

She calls
other names
and slowly the fight
           goes out
in all of us
open our maths books
           with no fuss
but I notice she looks down
at her screen
       as she teaches
and later
when I pass her desk
I spy the seating plan.

She sees me looking
       gives a wink

and now
I start to think
I might just like
                her
way more
than I ever liked
                sir.

MY FAULT

I used to think
when people fought
they used mean words
    like kids at school
    when they shout and swear
    and call each other
             nasty names.

But now I know
        there's other ways to fight.

Sometimes
it means

silence

saying absolutely nothing at all
so the silence becomes jagged

like little pieces of glass

cutting into you.

Other times

a door closes

with a **BANG**

a pot clatters

too loudly

a look that says

'I don't even like you anymore'

and inside

my tummy twists and turns

'cos a little voice is whispering

it's your fault

it's your fault

it's your fault

maybe if they had a   different

better

tidier

nicer

kinder

smarter

daughter

things wouldn't be

like this.

And I start to think

MUST   TRY   HARDER

but what if

I have no **SUPERPOWERS**

after all?

FEAR MOVES IN

Feel something move through me
                        claws sharp and pointy
till it finds a place
to rest.

Fear decides to build
its nest
inside
    my heart.

ALONE

The sea's a muddy grey
                today
waves choppy
                like a ploughed field
where gulls flock
                in search of food.

I'm sitting on the rocks
sketching *Girl Awesome*
who's wearing
                cool clothes
                        her cool sisters
helped her choose.

Sunny swims in circles
                slow and steady
like he knows
I'm not in the mood
                for fancy jumps and twists

'cos today all I need
is to know
           he's there.
Cian's off doing family stuff
probably fighting
           and squabbling
with those siblings
           the ones I wish were mine.

If I had little sisters
I'd love them following me around
copying everything I did
taking my things
           mini-mes
or older ones
           like Mya's
who I could talk to
about the stuff
I can't say to Mam,
           to anyone.

But the thing I think I'd love the most

about having a sister

or a brother

would be the not always feeling so

ALONE.

SUCCESS

Ms Flynn marches us all outside

               even though it's drizzling.

Says we have to

               'do some trials

               for the school athletics team'

(I never knew we had one)

               'as the county finals

               are only a month away!'

The sporty kids

are keen to show what they can do

as Ms Flynn blows her whistle

to send them charging round the cones

boys first

               then girls.

I don't come last

       but somewhere in the middle

and no one's surprised

when the usual kids

      make the cut

        and strut

  around

pretending to be surprised

    like they didn't know all along

they'd succeed.

Then she makes us try the long jump

        which I'm rubbish at

but when it's Cian's turn

he runs so fast

on those *lanky* legs

then jumps

      so that he's flying through the air

like his feet have wings attached

        that carry him

          on and on

like *magic*

further than anyone else

      can go.

And even the sporty kids are quiet

when Ms Flynn gets him to jump again

to make sure it's not a one-off

a fluke.

When he goes even further

Ms Flynn looks like she might burst

or worse

hug him

She's like a cat starting to purr

her eyes already sparkling with his success

shimmering with the promise

of all the shiny medals

he might win

for her.

LOST

I used to think that being lost
meant you didn't know
where you were.
Like once in Tesco
when I was small
    and wandered off
couldn't find Mam anywhere.

The voice on the Tannoy
said my name
my age
and the colour of my hair
my coat.

And a woman
I didn't know
brought me to Mam
who squeezed me
       too tight

and

was sad

    and happy

and cross

all at the same time

like she couldn't pick

just one.

But lost isn't always like that.

Sometimes you can feel
      LOST
when you are with people you know.

Sometimes you can feel
      LOST
when you know

exactly

where you are.

ENGINE HOUSE

Cian's house
hums
    and hisses
        and huffs
like a big old engine where all the parts
want to do their own thing
while making
    as much noise
as possible.

We're sitting on the living room floor
doing homework for Ms C
writing a diary entry
as if we were like Stanley
in *Holes*
stuck in a place
where bad kids are sent
to make them good
again.

Beside us

The Bean's little brother

roars at the telly

as he shoots aliens

that don't want to die.

The words come easily into my head

and Cian types them up

on his mam's laptop

one for me

    then one for him

just different enough

    that no one will know

they both came

from inside my head.

A radio **crackles** in the kitchen

    the clicky-clacky sounds

of someone emptying a dishwasher.

Upstairs one sister shouts
'Give it back'

then another
'No way.
You gave it to me
it's mine.'

Louder now
'Not for keeps
only a loan
it's mine.
You're so mean!'

A door **BANGS**
'Maaaaam' one sister screams
so loud the house shakes
and the row spills
     and rolls
        and tumbles
down the stairs.

'Sorry'

Cian says

looking like he wants to escape

with the aliens

       into the TV screen

and stay there

       forever.

'It's okay'

I say

'cos here I get to see

what a family

    should be.

Here I get to pretend

it all belongs

    to me.

PUZZLED

Ms C perches on the edge of her desk
    where she can see
what everyone is doing
    can reach each corner of the room
with those clever eyes
that seem to flit
    and flick
and make us all sit
so still
we could be made of ice
except those eyes are way too warm
for that.

If I drew her
she'd be a bird
her pink and purple flowy skirt
    fabulous feathers
        unfurling
to the ground

and her springy curls
    small downy wisps
that frame her face.

'Mya, let's hear your homework'
she says.

Mya 'ah-hum's
        fakes shyness
then sits a little taller in her chair
and in her best sugary stage-school voice
reads out her work.

When she's done
she waits
    expecting the usual praise
Mr K used to pour
on her.

Instead
Ms C tilts her head

this way
     then that
scrunches up her nose
and while her voice says
'Good effort'
her eyes
   her face
say Mya's work
is actually
nothing special.

Then those clever eyes
flicker round the room
looking for a place to land.
They come to settle
        on me.

But today
   it's okay
no tightness
   in my tummy

no ache
    in my head
'cos The Bean helped me
learn it off
till every word
was **BURNT** into my brain.

I say it loud
        sing it like a song
barely glancing down
knowing   exactly
what comes next.
When I've finished
Ms C looks at me
like those eyes can see
    more than my face
can peer deep inside
    me.

'Lovely work, Ró' she says
and talks about

'the raw emotion in my words'
how they
        'ooze with feeling'
but all the time
those clever eyes keep watching me
like my dad
when he's trying to get the squares
of the Rubik's cube
        lined up.

All day long
Ms C watches me
                like I'm a puzzle
she's determined
to figure out.

OLDER, NOT WISER

'That one's been on this earth before'
my granny used to say
when I was small
and she'd find me
listening
           to things
I wasn't meant to hear.

But listening

helped me understand

    learn about the world

    and how things work.

now

when I catch

those jagged snippets

    angry whispers late at night

it only makes me feel

             confused

like I don't know that much

about anything

after all.

TOGETHER

I have no clue

how two people

are meant

to fit

together.

WAR WOUNDS

I dip my hand into the bucket
of slimy silver fish
         all dead eyes
         and creepy smiles
that Pat has brought with us.

Through the fog we move
to the rhythm
of Pat's smooth and steady
swishy strokes.

'Look at this fella' I say
lifting out a fish
hold its whiskery little mouth
    up at The Bean
pinch the edges of the *jelly* lips
      between my fingers
so the mouth wobbles
    open then closed
like it's trying to speak.

'Get off' Cian says
nudging me away
'That's kinda freaky, Ró'
but he's laughing all the same.

Then he shoves his hand in
pulls a whopper out.

'I'M THE BIG FISH AROUND HERE!'
he says
a silly voice
that suits the fish
and now I'm laughing too.

'Easy there' Pat says
pulling up the oars.

We sit and watch the fog
hang over the water
like it will never move
waiting

quiet now
till Sunny appears
gentle through the **sea**
close to the boat
a kind brown eye
our welcome.

Pat shows us how to hold the fish
'Like an ice-cream cone' he says.

The round nose rises up
mouth open
a velvet pink tongue
and chains of needle teeth.

Pat throws a fish
and it slides in.
Then another and another
Sunny moving closer
with each one.

My turn now.

He comes near

hold the fish like Pat said

then let it drop in.

And feel so good

       like I've achieved

       something big

           from doing this one small thing.

'What's that?' I say

spotting a cut

a curve of little marks in his skin.

'He's a wild creature' Pat says

'they fight

sometimes bite each other.'

He shrugs

'That's nature

CRUEL and *beautiful*

       both at once.'

When the bucket is empty

we row back to shore.

Sunny *swims* beside us for a bit

then turns and flips

 and heads away

  disappearing into endless grey.

All the way back

I think about Pat's words

and wonder if they apply to people too.

Could it be true

 that we can also be

two different

 opposite

things

 both at once?

EXQUISITE

Sitting on the low wall

it's one of those days

that promises rain

    that never comes

like everything is stuck

    exactly as it is.

The Bean's off practising the long jump

        'No time to waste' Ms Flynn said

        marching him away

        to join the sporty kids.

He rolled his eyes

    just for me

    like he didn't want to go.

But now I think maybe he did

'cos he's laughing and messing

with the other boys

who never used to talk

to us.

I'm sketching **Girl Awesome**
her eyes wild and wide
mouth open
    in a comic **O**
ready to scream
white fingers clutching metal
as the rollercoaster cart
begins to drop.

Behind
her *awesome* sisters
start to squeal
with all that nervous fun
    still to come.

'That's exquisite' Ms C says
standing beside me
staring down at my work.
I try to pull it towards me
but it's too late.

'How'd you learn to draw like that?'
those clever eyes rise from the page
                settle on my face.

'YouTube mostly' I say and shrug
hoping she won't ask to see more.

'All that detail
really is amazing' she says
and smiles
        her eyes alive and thinking
like she's just slipped
                and clicked
another tiny piece
of the puzzle
        that is me
into its proper place.

ASKING ALEXA

Alexa says **exquisite** means

> **beautiful** and **outstanding**
> and **excellent**.

Big words that describe big things
big words that feel

WAY

TOO

BIG

for me.

ANOTHER ME

Last night I dreamed there was **another me**
a mirror image
a girl who *walked*

        and *talked*
        and *looked*
        and *thought*

like me.
Someone to share things with
this room
    this house
        this life.
Someone *just for me*.

When I woke she was gone
        into little wisps of dreams
           I couldn't catch.

And now I miss her
even though she never was

except inside my head

never really lived

except inside my **dreams**.

THE PRINCESS AND THE PEA

Step from the shower and wrap myself in a giant towel.

A smaller one to squeeze the water from my hair. Start to pat my body dry. Arms. Legs. Then chest. Where I notice *it*. Something small, stuck under my skin, like the princess discovering that *little pea*.

Check the other side. Another one. Smaller. Wipe the steam from the mirror and examine my body. **TINY BULGES** that were never there before. **TINY BULGES** I don't want.

How do I make them **DISAPPEAR?**

This wasn't part of my plan.

To. Keep. Everything. The. Same.

SETTLING A SCORE

Ms C decides a Friday spelling test
will become a thing.

Perched on her desk
she seems to pluck the words
from the air that hums and *fizzes*
around her.

Lots of empty desks today
as the sporty kids have gone
with Ms Flynn
to try to win
as many medals as they can
at the county finals.

The first few spellings are easy

set

sun

to make you think
you're not as **STUPID**

      as you are.
But then

      bigger words
I know the meaning of
but with tricky sounds

words I can't picture in my head
can't decide on the right letters

      that go into them.

Even though I've tried
to learn some of them before
it's like my brain

      couldn't find a way
to let them in.

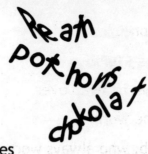

Leave blank spaces

can't keep up

WORDS and **WORDS** and more **WORDS**

getting all mashed up inside my head.

Ask Ms C for the toilet

'CAN'T YOU WAIT TILL WE'RE DONE?'

I shake my head

scrunch up my nose

and wiggle in my seat

    like I'm about to burst

           'Hurry then' she says

but I don't

I take my time

    linger at the window

        loll against the sink

    loiter in the hallway

so when I get back

the test is done.

Ms C got them to swap over
to correct the work
except Jakob, who always works with me, has
gone to the finals.

'I have yours' Mya says
and slides it over
making a big deal
    like she desperately wants
    Ms C to notice
the **BIG** numbers
she has written on my test

4/30

in her annoying neat handwriting.

'Hard luck' Mya says
smiling at me.

When I try to take the page

she presses her hand down

     pinning it to the desk

daring me to make a fuss.

I pull it away

and the paper tears

Ms C spins round

     asks what's wrong

but Mya has already turned away

and it looks like I've ripped my test

        on purpose.

Wait for Ms C to get cross

to shout

or say something

     about my rubbish score

but she doesn't

just lets those clever eyes

rest on me

for the longest while

then turns to talk to someone else.

WINNING AND LOSING

Gold and silver medals
HANG
   and **CLANG**
like *jewels* around The Bean's neck
and seem to make him taller
than he was before.

Kids swarm around
like he's some Olympian
   back from The Games
not just a boy

who can jump **FURTHER** **HIGHER** *better*
than the rest
not just that quiet lanky boy
   who has always been
my friend.

A LETTER TO MYSELF

Ms C wants us to write a letter

to our older selves

when we are eighteen

and all grown up

wants us to put it in an envelope

keep it somewhere safe

not open it

till six years have passed

except I don't want to think

of myself like that

don't want to be

all big and old

what can I say

to this girl I will become?

That everything

will be okay?

That maybe

you won't feel so **stupid** then?

But that would be

a **BIG** fat lie

so instead

I fold the page

slip it

into the envelope

having written

not a single word.

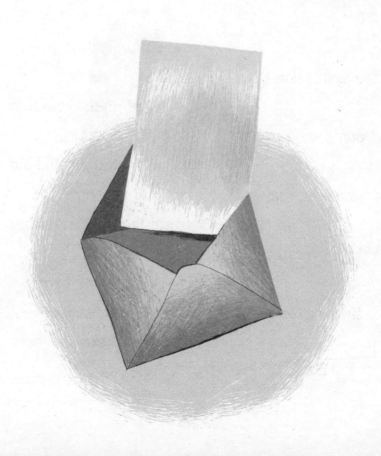

WAITING

Sitting on the low wall
    waiting for The Bean.

Today
    he doesn't come.

GRAVITY

Mam's eyes are **puffy**
with tiny red veins
running through the white
    when I come downstairs.

Her hands are clamped
around her tea
like there's no longer
    any gravity
and that mug's the only thing
tethering her to the earth.

'Where's Dad?' I ask
no sign of pancake making.

                'Gone to work.'
'On a Sunday?'

           'An emergency' she says
              not looking up.

And I wonder how a garage

that shuts on Sundays

can have an emergency.

Not like Mya's dad

    a fancy doctor

who works all sorts of hours.

I make the pancakes

but the batter's too **LUMPY**

    sticks to the pan

'cos I forgot to smear the butter

and too much baking powder

makes them taste all salty.

Leave a few in the oven

for Dad when he gets back

but when he does

it's nearly dark

    and somehow he looks smaller

    when he comes in the door

        like he's got some invisible weight

strapped to his back

that's pushing him down and down.

When I check the oven

it's empty

Mam's already thrown the pancakes in the bin.

CHEST PASSES

I throw the ball at The Bean

        he flings it back

as we side-step

        up and down the gym

the ball moving back and forth

        between us

a **connection**

        that nearly makes us

us again

        except nearly isn't enough

and I don't know how

        to make us

us again.

Ms C blows the whistle

        we all stop moving

The Bean holds the ball

        his eyes slide across

on to my shirt

where those annoying little **BuMPS**
poke out   **UNWANTED**

tiny peaks under my polo

heat rises in my cheeks

as he looks away

I quickly fold my arms   high up

try to stay like that

but it's too late to hide

what he's already seen.

COVERING UP

Find some plasters
    in the bathroom cupboard
take two big ones
and peel the tricky
    sticky tabs off.

Cover up one little **BUMP**
then the other.

Put a vest on
then my polo shirt
and remind myself
to
NEVER
EVER
take
my
jumper

at
school
again.

ANONYMOUS

Ms C asks me to wait

    wants to have a word

as the others head for break.

I stand beside her desk

as she rummages in the drawer

pulls out the torn spelling test

now magically back together

      Sellotaped across the middle

and I'm wondering how

'cos I'm a hundred per cent sure

I threw it in the bin.

        'I wanted to chat about this' she says

          pushing it towards me

            like it's a part

              of me

            one I don't want.

        'These words were hard for you?'

ALL WORDS are hard for me

I want to say

but don't

    say anything.

She looks at my untidy writing

messy squiggles

    like ugly **STAINS** on the page

                'Maybe it's

                a bit the same

                with reading?'

I shake my head

'That's not mine'

I say

    remembering I never wrote my name

'It's someone else's'

she pushes it closer

                'You think so?'

those clever eyes watching me

    intensely

but I stay firm

stare at the board behind her

and let the silence build up

    like a wall between us

till she decides

to let me go

but inside I know

    of course

        she knows

I'm lying.

BABY CLOTHES

Mam helps me sort my room.
She wants to peel
the big tree sticker
and the faded woodland animals
from my wall.

'I put those up before you were born'
she says
    'before we knew
if you'd be
a girl
    or boy.'
She gets that look in her eyes
the one that usually means
she's going to hug me
       too tight
but not today.

Mam is right

the stickers are too babyish
and even though I know
I can't stay her little girl forever
part of me wants to keep them up
so nothing has to change.

We lift down a wicker basket
from above the wardrobe.
'I remember you wearing these'
she says
taking out tiny purple dungarees
    with daisies on the pockets.
Then she oohs and aahs
over the baby onesies
that seem to come
    in every colour
      of the rainbow
holds one up to her face
takes a deep breath   in
'Yeah' she says
closing her eyes

'it's still there
        that **yummy**
            scrummy
        baby smell'
but now I can't tell
if she's really happy
        or really sad
and I realise I never knew
those two things
could be so close together.

'Charity shop?'
I say
        already thinking
I can use the basket
for my art things.

She nods
        adds them to the pile.
'I thought it would be different'
she says still staring at the clothes.

I ask her what she means
'This. All of it.'
she rolls her eyes
           'Life.
It seemed easier back then.
Simpler.'

I think about saying something
but no words feel right
when I try them in my head
so I say nothing.

'Right' she says
'will we tackle those stickers?'

Later
      when I bag up all the stuff
to give away
I notice the purple dungarees
are missing from the pile.

Maybe I'm not the only one
who doesn't like
things to change.

Maybe I'm not the only one
who wants to keep everything
the same.

GLASS WINDOWS

There are big white pages on our desks
    when we come in from lunch.
Tubes of paint and jars of messy brushes
    dotted here and there
a box of stained aprons
    in the middle of the room.

'Tidy Towns is running a competition'
Ms C says
'to design a stained-glass window
for the community hall.'

She mentions some lady
    an artist with a fancy name
who will choose the winner
then   like **magic**
turn the picture into glass.

And now my brain is **bubbling**

bursting *brimming* **BOILING**

with ideas

of how to fill that page

colours   pictures   feelings

simmer in my head

they *shimmer* and *shine*

        and sing to me

till I feel like I'll explode

so I take a brush

        and start to mix the paint.

COLOURS

Brush dips into paint
colour swirls

outline already sketched
waiting to be filled

with a million shades
a sea that isn't blue

but mustard and mandarin
aqua and ash

sunflower and saffron
fuchsia and flamingo

charcoal and coffee
copper and cobalt

olive and opal
salmon and sapphire

so many colours
to make one ocean
come alive
in the sunlight   of my mind

dancing on the breeze
of my **IMAGINATION**

out of the rainbow water
Sunny rises high

use my fingertips
texture his skin with mine

so he becomes
a beautiful soaring creature

that's now a part
          of me.

USED TO BE

Today I brought chocolate sweets
for The Bean to eat at lunch
hoping he might
sit with me
    again
hoping he might
like me
    again.

'Thanks' he says
ripping the packet open
and munching on the sweets
like nothing's changed between us
when to me it feels like
           everything
has.

Jakob comes over
asks if he wants to be in goal

The Bean offers him the sweets
      pours half the bag into his hand
and they run across the yard
so easy with each other
exactly like
      we
used to be.

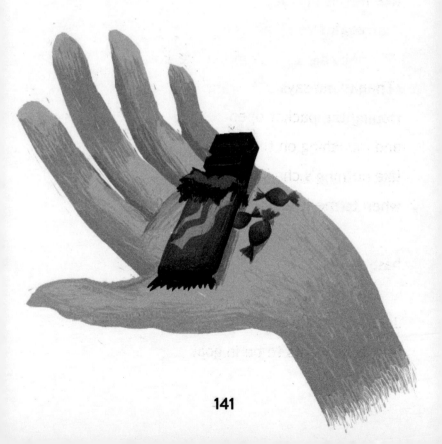

JUST CIAN

As we head home
I call him over
    ask if something's wrong.

'Wrong?' he says
like I'm speaking
a different language
'Nothing's wrong' he says
    not able to look me in the eye
acting like he doesn't want
to talk to me.

'But, Ró' he says
'stop calling me that.'

'Heh?' I say
not getting it.

'The Bean.

Don't call me that anymore.
Just Cian
okay?'

'Okay' I say
not used to hearing
        prickles in his voice
not used to him
        being **SALTY**
with me.

Spend most of the evening
in my room
wondering what it is
I did wrong.

GOING SOLO

I do my homework

on my own tonight

        no Cian to help me out.

I write the words

into my English copy

        my left hand **SMEARING** ink

                as it moves across the

                        page

not caring

if the words are right

    or wrong

not bothered

if the letters are

    okay

or what Ms C will say.

'Cos something hurts inside

a little **spark** of pain

slowing growing
    into an angry **FLAME**
that stops me caring
    about my work
stops me caring
    about anything.

FREE

Grey clouds
stained with orange

like smoke
they climb across the sky

I watch Sunny swimming
in a slate-grey sea

wonder how it would feel
to be that free

wonder how it would be
if that was me.

UNITY

Open my bedroom door
a tiny **CRACK**

something woke me
a noise

a **BANG**

or maybe just the need to pee.

Hear them arguing downstairs
mean words bounce back and forth
like balls on a tennis court
each a little worse
than the one before.

If I was brave
I'd go down there
shout at them   to stop
be nicer

to each other.

147

Instead
    I close the door
creep back to bed
and imagine I'm not here
but swimming in a **warm warm** sea
    with Sunny
separate
but *together*
just him and me
    in complete
unity.

WIDER THAN THE SEA

When Ms C asks me

      to stay behind

I already know

      what it's about.

             'This homework'

                she says

          my English copy open

          on the homework page

    'You struggled with the writing?'

I look at the muddled

        messy

marks I've made.

Before

      I'd want to rub them out

        make them disappear

          feel embarrassed by my work

but now

      I tell myself

I
don't
care.
I shrug
         not wanting to answer her
         not wanting to let her see
         one inch
                  inside of me.
                                    'You know, Ró
                                    you have this **LIGHT**
                                    this golden **LIGHT**
                                    inside of you.'
                                    She's staring now
                                    her eyes fixed on mine.
                                    'I've seen your sketches
                  that *beautiful* painting of the dolphin.
                                    Inside here—'
                                    she taps my head
'is vast and **wonderful** and **amazing**.
                  It's . . . it's higher than the stars
                                    it's wider than . . .'

she looks around
out towards the Atlantic
'IT'S WIDER THAN THE SEA.
This thing with words
is tiny
a little blip in your big blue ocean.
We can overcome it.
YOU can overcome it.
But here's the thing, Ró
how your brain works
also makes you you.
Gives you all this *amazing* talent
lets you see the world
in such a *unique* way.'

I want to tell her
                that isn't how it feels.
                to me it's **HUGE** and dark and
                ENDLESS
                spilling over everything
but I stay quiet.
                        'Maybe we could get your parents in
                                        for a chat
                        think about getting you assessed.'
'No' I say too loud
'They wouldn't want that.'
                                'But I think we can help—'
'No' I'm shaking my head
thinking I don't want them
to know my **STUPID** brain
doesn't work
can't do
the simple things
everyone else's   can
        don't want the world to see
                the broken bits of me.

'Ró, I really think . . .'

She gets an envelope from her desk

'Just give them this, okay?'

I take it from her

and leave without a word.

Have no intention

of giving it

to anyone.

WAITING

Water pale blue
            today
a hazy winter sun sits low
like it's too lazy
to climb into the sky
        burn the clouds away.

Scan the waves
hoping for a glimpse
of Sunny
thinking that each curve of wave
each nose of foam
        is him.

Pat's down at his boat.
When I ask where Sunny is
he shrugs

says he hasn't seen him
in a while
'Who knows where
wild creatures go.'

On the rocks
    I sit
wait
    till my eyes
get tired of looking
wait
    till heavy clouds
roll in
    and misty rain
begins to fall
wait
    till my hair is wet

and my fingers
   have gone **NuMB**.

But all that time I'm waiting
and hoping,
         Sunny doesn't come.

BUTTERFLY WINGS

I use my brush
    to make the **WAVES**
        rise up
swirl it round
    to show the movement
of the sea
so it becomes
    a living
        breathing
entity.

Some of us stay after school
        to finish off our entries.
'That's really cool'
I say to Mya
'cos hers so is.
She's painted a girl
    with butterfly wings
except   when you look closer

you see the wings

    are torn and tattered

will never let the girl

lift off the ground.

Mya looks up

    like maybe I don't mean

what I say.

'Thanks' she says

when she's sure I do

'Yours is cool too' she adds

like the words

    hurt her mouth.

A car horn beeps outside

    I recognise the fancy car

Mya's dad must be on a call

'cos he's busy

talking to himself

    arms waving in the air.

Mya stands up quickly
        starts to pack away her things
the car horn toots again
three   sharp   blasts
                        close together now
she knocks her brush jar over
spilling dirty brown water
on to the edge of her painting.
'Noooo' she says
just staring at the desk
'I've ruined it.'

I grab a rag
        wipe the water off
        before it spreads
then carefully peel the picture
from the table.
'You'll barely notice
        once it's dry.'

The horn blasts again
Mya takes her bag and coat
'Thanks, Ró' she says
like she really means it
and hurries out of the door.

From the window
I watch her go.
Her dad doesn't seem to notice
as she climbs into the car
keeps talking on his phone
like she isn't even there.
The car zooms off
too fast
and I look again at Mya's picture
her butterfly girl
who'll never get to try those wings
who'll never learn
to fly.

FRACTURED

Once
when I was small
I fell from the monkey bars
in the park.

Remember hearing the bone go
   snap
in my right arm
pain like a needle
   that becomes a knife
   then the sharpest sword
      growing
till it's **bigger**
than everything.

I used to think
it was only bones
that could snap
   like that

but now I know

that other things

can fracture too

but silently

so you don't notice

till it's too late

till the damage

is already

done.

BOY-WEIRD

I'm heading home
when Mya falls into step
beside me.

'No lift today?' I say.

'No' she says
like she's relieved
    about that.

'No Cian?' she asks.

'No' I say
not at all relieved
    about that.

We glance over
to the playing field
where the sporty kids

are practising
Cian in the thick
    of everything.

'He's gone all weird' I say.

'Ah, that's boy-weird' she says
smiling at me.
'My sister Sarah says
it's a thing.
She also says
there's only one cause
that brings it on.'

Cian and Jakob
are pushing each other now
shoulder to shoulder
trying to prove
who is the strongest.

'He likes you' she says.

'Heh?' I say, confused.
'Well, he doesn't act like it.'

'No. Not likes you.
He "likes you"'
and she uses her fingers
to make those silly
air marks
then she shouts over
'Hey, Cian' she yells
and when the boys look up
she lifts my hand
and waves it
at them.
Cian goes all awkward
and mutters a quick 'hi'
then turns away.
'See' Mya says
boy-weird.
'He definitely likes you.'

'How long does it last
        this boy-weird?' I ask
'cos I'm wondering if I'll ever
get my best friend back.

'Sarah says
it doesn't last long
only till they move on
to "liking" someone else.
Though my mum disagrees.
She says it lasts forever.'

MISSING

I type Sunny's name
> into the box
and a load of dolphin pics
> and links pop up.

I spot his name
> and click on it
but there's too many **WORDS**
> for me to read.

I hit the sound symbol
and a robot voice
begins to talk
'Concern growing over local dolphin.
Fears are rising
for the bottlenose dolphin
known locally as Sunny
who has made Kilbeglin bay
his home.'

The computer voice
tells me
local fishermen
haven't seen him
in almost two weeks
say he might
have travelled further
for food
because of winter tides.

Some expert fella says
the most likely thing
is 'old age'
but I stop listening
turn the stupid voice off
not wanting to hear
what I know he's going to say.

RIVER

Sadness

twists

and turns

like a **RIVER**

through

our house

it flows

from Dad

to Mam

then on

to me.

I want

to make that

RIVER stop

but how can

one girl

hold all that

sadness

back

how can

she stop

herself

being

washed

away?

KINTSUGI . . .

Ms C tells us

is the Japanese craft

of fixing broken things.

Smashed and cracked and split

cups and bowls and plates

made whole again.

Tree-sap and rice glue

stick the broken pieces

back together

then gold or silver is melted

into precious shiny streams

to cover the damaged seams

of these broken things

that are now

more beautiful

than they were before.

I wish I knew Kintsugi

'cos there's so many things

I'd like to fix

so many things

I'd try to make better

than they were

before.

WANTING

The community hall
    hums and heaves
with the sound
of too many kids.

A patchwork of greys and greens
of navies and wines
    sixth-class kids
    from all the schools
jammed in.

A group of parents
stands around the silver urn
taking turns to pour the tea
    into plastic cups
and looking like
they don't know what to say
to each other.

On the low stage
three pictures are lined up
perched on wooden easels
		like real artists use
each covered by a silky cloth
		so no one can see
what's underneath.

'Can you hear me?
Can everyone hear me?'
A small woman
with big glasses
taps the microphone
		making it screech and squeal
and crackle round the room.

Behind her
someone fiddles with an amp
until the crackling
		becomes a piercing whistle
			then a dying whine.

'Welcome all' she says
'I'm Caroline Hughes
local councillor
and this is Kimberly Abebe
our resident artist
and judge for today.'

A woman with purple hair
smiles down at us
she takes the mic
spouts all the usual stuff
　　how amazing the entries were
　　　　how hard it was to pick the winner
　　how we're all winners really
　　　　for putting ourselves out there
　　for taking part
blah-dee-blah-blah-blah.
I stop listening
　　watch the ceiling
　　　　where a crumpled helium balloon
shaped like a number three

has tried to escape
almost but not quite
succeeding.

As I'm wondering
if some little kid
bawled and bawled
as it floated up
and out of reach
everyone starts to clap.
The first painting is uncovered
a boy from another school
goes up to claim third prize.

Second place next.
Straight away
I recognise it
Mya's beautiful butterfly girl.
As her name's called out
and she climbs on to the stage
I feel all mixed up inside

like hot and cold together
'cos I'm jealous
and not jealous
trying to be happy for Mya
as she smiles
and takes her prize
but I can't.

My hands clap
for Mya

but

my heart blisters
for me.

RESULT

The third cloth is pulled off
and even as I hear my name
     see Sunny leaping into the air
I can't believe

I've
      won?

I've
      won . . .

I've
      won!

FLOATING

Know exactly how
that helium balloon
must have felt
as I float
on to the stage
    like I'm the one
full of bubbling air
    like I'm the one
        escaping.
Remember now
what Ms C
said to me
maybe my brain
really is

WIDER

than the **SEA**?

VENOM

Feels funny
so many eyes watching
everyone clapping
            for me.

In the sea of faces
I spot my dad
        beaming
and clapping
like his life depends on it.

The artist woman is speaking
says how 'stunning'
the winning paintings are
says she has written
'a short appraisal
of each one.'
A sheet of paper
is shoved into my hand

someone steers me

towards the mic

and the hall goes quiet

people waiting

watching

as I realise

what I'm supposed to do.

I stare at the words

where all the letters

work against me

    like snakes

they slide and slither

across the page

ready to bite

sink their venom   in.

Search for words to cling to

             ones I recognise

try to whisper

but the mic makes me too loud

'the . . . eh . . . use of . . .'
look at the audience.
Ms C is near the back
her face all tight
    like paper
scrunched into a ball.

I try to read more words
'tone . . . in . . . the . . . this'
glance up again.
Eyes watching.
Some look away
    embarrassed
for me.
See my dad's face
    disappointed
in me.

Ms C starts to move
pushing through the crowd
and now it feels like

someone's taken all the air away

filled my mouth with sand

    like I'm trapped

DEEP beneath the ocean

no light   no air   no sound.

Let the page slip from my hand

        have to find the surface

hear someone call my name

but my legs are already moving

        have to leave this place.

ESCAPE

Running but don't know where I'm going
running to leave them all behind
running to stop the hurting
running to escape myself
running to become
anyone
but
me.

TOO BIG

Feels like
everything that was inside
is now out.

Feels like
everyone has seen
the broken bits of me.

Feels like
no matter how far I run
it won't ever be far enough.

'Cos now it's all too big
                              to ever fit back in.

AFLOAT

I stand
a tiny
    nothing
on the rocks
one speck against this big ocean
that wraps itself
halfway round the world.

I watch each rise and dip of wave
know Sunny must be out there
           somewhere
wonder if he's missing me.
Remember that moment
when I touched his skin
and know that finding him
is the only thing
that can make
the aching stop

make me feel
not broken.

Pat's boat is tied up
against the pier.
I walk over
    and climb in.

SPLASH-SWISH

I step into the centre

to keep the balance

untie the fat rope

from the rusty metal ring

thread the oars

through the horse-shoe holders

>> and push off.

Splash– swish

>> Splash– swish

Splash– swish

Find the rhythm

the way Pat said

my back is to the ocean

and with each stroke

I watch the town

begin to shrink

>> sink into the distance.

Splash– *swish*
   Splash– *swish*
Splash– *swish*

Head out towards the headland
where I've seen him go.
Didn't know before
a single thought
could be everything.

Splash– *swish*
   Splash– *swish*
Splash– *swish*

A single moment
will fix everything.

HOPE

With each *dip* of oar
the ache begins to *shrivel*
and hope starts to **GROW**.

JUST COME

I round the headland
pull the oars up into the boat
and wait for Sunny to appear.

Wonder if he senses
that I'm here
am sure that he will come
once he does.

Keep watching the water
willing him to just be there.

Something stirs
    a *splash* near the rocks
a fat seal slides into the *sea*
lifts his head
then swims away
not interested
    in me.

Drops of icy rain
start to fall
and sit like tiny beads
on my jumper.
I feel cold now
but I won't go
till he's here.

'Just come'
I keep saying in my head
    like maybe he can hear
even though I know that's stupid.

'Just come'
I shout it now
angry with him
    with myself
        with everything.

'Just come'

I say

whispering

'cos I already know

        he won't.

HOPELESS

With each **drop** of rain
hope begins to **SHRIVEL**
the ache starts to **GROW**.

DISTANCE

Shadows come
creeping in along the water
to take away the light
and leave me in this grey place
    that space between night
          and day
where I don't know
    what each shape is
each sound
    is strange to me.
I take the oars
start to row
turn the boat around
wanting to be home now
    with Dad in the kitchen
        helping him make tea.

I've gone further than I thought
and even though I heave

with all my might

it feels like I'm not moving

like some weird force

is holding me in place.

I stop rowing

pick a spot on land

     the tallest tree up on the hill

and watch it

keep watching without blinking

realise the boat's still moving

the current pulling me

        out into the **DARKNESS**

away from where I want to go.

Take the oars again

work harder

pull and pull and pull

Splash– *swish*

     Splash– *swish*

Splash– *swish*

make the oars go faster

Splash– **swish**

      Splash– **swish**

Splash– **swish**

      make my arms work harder

Splash– **swish**

      Splash– **swish**

Splash– **swish**

but no matter how hard I try

when I look up again

      find my tree

I'm even further away

than I was before.

REWIND

I drop the oars

wrap my arms around my legs

and   wish *wish* **wish**

that I could go back

retrace my steps

so I didn't end up here

       like this.

And I'm crying now

     'cos it's almost **DARK**

     'cos I'm cold

     and sopping wet.

But mostly I'm crying

'cos I might not

get home

ever

and the worst thing is

I know it's all

my own

silly **STUPID** fault.

DARK SKY . . .

black black
    sea

a heaving
    breathing thing

that doesn't want
    me here.

I AM . . .

lost

BEACON

A tiny hum
    like a buzzing in my ear
        but getting bigger
            so I start to hope
                it might be outside of
                me.

A small light
    shining in the distance
        but getting bigger
            so I start to hope
                it might be coming
                towards
                      me.

BIGGER THAN I AM

Turn towards the light
wave my arms
and shout
but that whining noise
DROWNS me out.

Take the oar
and stand up
hold it high
like a flag in the air
the boat **WOBBLES**
sit back down
shout louder
'I'm here
I'm over here'
keep shouting and waving
waving and shouting
try to make myself
bigger than I am

and watch that growing light

willing it

to come   for me.

SEARCH LIGHT

Light
growing **BRIGHT**
    like a rising sun
covering me
    with lovely yellow
light.

I BREATHE, I BREATHE, I BREATHE

The engine cuts
           lights and voices
moving
    calling
a long pole reaches
           grabs my boat
and pulls me
       in.

I'm lifted up
someone straps a life jacket on
then wraps a blanket
tight around me.

And my dad   my dad   crying
holds me like he's never going
to let go.

THE JOURNEY BACK

The fishing boat
chugs along the water
me and Dad
    on the deck
holding mugs of stewed tea.

Dad keeps touching my arm
    like he can't believe
      I'm real
    like he can't believe
      it's me.
              'You scared us, Ró'
              he says
              his voice different
              like it belongs to someone else
              'You shouldn't have run.'

I nod
but how do I tell him

I had no choice
		when everyone had seen
			inside of me
		when everyone had seen
			the worst of me.

				'Your teacher explained things'
					he looks at me
				'Why didn't you talk to us?'

Something stings inside
like skin splitting open
'But you never talk to me.'

					He looks surprised
						'What?
					Of course we—'

'You don't
I hear you fighting
being mean to each other.
You think I don't
but I do.

208

    I hear and see

                everything.'

I watch the churned-up water
fizzing behind the boat
feel the cold spray on my face
and I'm crying again now
    'cos I know I've started something
that can never be put back.

NEVER LETTING GO

Dad is quiet for a moment
staring into his tea

'Things with me
and your mam
it's . . . hard.
People don't stay the same
but change in tiny ways
till one day
you look up
and realise
everything is different
you're different
to when you started out.'

I think about me and Cian
kind of get what he means
'You stopped loving each other?'
I ask
even though I'm not sure

I want to hear the answer.

'Sometimes it's not about love
or maybe it's that love
isn't enough.'

'But you're parents
MY PARENTS
amn't I enough?'
He puts the mug down
holds my shoulders
in those big oily hands

'You are more
way more
than we ever wished for.
None of this is your fault.'

'But it is'
I'm shouting now
'If you leave then—'

'Leave?
I'm not leaving
I'm planning on trying
to fix things.

You know how good
I am at fixing engines
I keep going
don't give up
till I've tried everything.'
'But if you can't?
Sometimes
things can't
be fixed.'

'Then I wouldn't be leaving you
I'll never leave you.
Got it?'
I nod again
wanting every single word
to be true.

'Now your turn, Ró.'
'What?'

'Promise you'll let us help
with this school stuff?
Stop hiding it.'
I look at the lights of the town

growing bigger
as we get closer
to the shore
'I don't think it's that easy.'

'Your teacher says
you're a real brain box
that there's loads we can do
to make things better
for you.'
He's smiling now.
'That painting, Ró
I couldn't believe
that you did it.
God, I was so proud.'
And his eyes tell me
that he really means it
he's not lying.

My dad is proud of me.

I make the promise
and know it's one
        I have to keep.

The boat slows
        pulls into the pier
and Mam's there crying
        and waving from the quayside.

I climb down
and now I'm the one hugging like mad
            like my life depends on it
                like I'm never going

                        to let go.

WHAT EVERYONE CAN SEE

The water is still today
    sparkles like ice
        in the freezing air.
I don't come here much now
feels different
    without Sunny
        like a house left empty
        when the people move away.

No one's seen him in the bay
    since he disappeared
though Pat swore
he spotted him once
far out past the islands
    'Dozens of the fellas
    swimming in a pod!'
He was sure it was Sunny
    with the scar along his back
but I think he just said it

to make me feel better
　　to make me feel less sad.

We cycle back along the weir
and stop at Spar.

'There he is!' Mya says
as we park our bikes
against the wall.
Cian's coming out of the shop
munching Haribos.
'Here' he says
handing us a bag to share.
I take the sweets
know not to make a fuss.

We walk down towards the community hall
　　where the workmen are just finishing
and look up at the window
　　my painting turned to glass.
All those colours shimmering

in the low winter sun.

'It's so good, Ró' Cian says
still munching on his sweets.

'Yeah' Mya says. 'Imagine!
You did that!'

I look at Sunny up there
        forever leaping
from that rainbow-coloured sea.

And I smile now 'cos I know
it all came from me

from my brain

        that kind of really is

WIDER THAN THE SEA.

Author's Note

One of my earliest memories of school is a pair of big, heavy, swinging glass doors. After many attempts to escape out through them, always followed by the sinking sensation of being dragged back inside, I eventually gave in to my fate. What followed was years of trying to decipher all those wiggly, squiggly letters and numbers that never stayed in their place, symbols and markings that made no sense to me. All the other kids could do it, could read, could spell, could neatly replicate. Easy-peasy, for them.

So clearly the problem was me, right? When every message you receive is saying you can't achieve, you start to believe that to be true. It becomes who and what you are. And, well, someone has to be the child bumping along at the bottom of the class, don't they?

Luckily for me, fate did its thing. Just as frustration and perished self-esteem had begun to metamorphosize into bad behaviour, a new teacher with a kind heart and a sharp eye arrived. She cut through the dyslexic ice and slowly the world started to become a different place. Words began to mean something and when joined together I realised they could lead you to all kinds of places, let you peek into other people's lives and worlds. With help and a lot of practice, I had learned to read. These things that had for so long perplexed me now started to fascinate me.

Later, I went on to study Literature and returned to the classroom as an English teacher, something that would have seemed completely impossible for the child-me. And when, more recently, my little boy asked me why the words kept moving on the page, I wasn't in the least bit surprised, but I knew exactly how to help him.

ACKNOWLEDGEMENTS

To everyone at The Gresham Writers' Group, especially John Givens, Caroline Madden, Andrew Hughes and Antain McLoughlin, thank you for your endless support and encouragement. Thanks to Sue McGlone, Michelle Kenney and Lisa Bradley for your friendship and to all the talented Scribblers.

A big thank you to my lovely agent Sara O'Keeffe, for believing, and then weaving her magic, always with the kindest touch. Thanks to all the team at Hachette, especially Rachel Wade for embracing Ró and Sunny from the start, and to Jenna Mackintosh, for whom nothing is ever too much trouble. Thanks also to George Ermos for creating such a beautiful cover and all the gorgeous illustrations throughout.

I am incredibly grateful to all the Ms Cs who have helped me over the years. You made all the difference.

Thanks to my parents for *everything*, and to Fiona for the spellings (and so much more.)

For their patience, love and constant inspiration, thank you Oisín, Aoibheann, Sadbh and Fionn. And finally, thanks to Stewart for Thursdays.

Serena Molloy was born in Wexford, Ireland, and is an English teacher who has taught in different schools across the UK. She settled in Galway with her family, where she can see the sea every day. As a mum of four, her house is always noisy but never, ever dull.

Serena endured her own struggle with dyslexia as a child, until an inspirational teacher changed her life. Her novels are a celebration of neurodiversity, empathy and the power to change.

Twitter: @happy_scribbler

Instagram: @serena_molloy

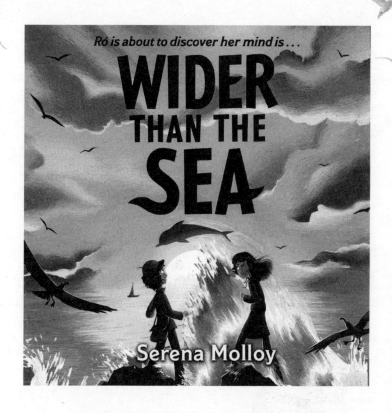

Ró is about to discover her mind is . . .

WIDER THAN THE SEA

Serena Molloy

ALSO AVAILABLE AS AN AUDIOBOOK!